Contents

Ladybird

Cover illustration by Leonie Shearing

A catalogue record for this book is available from the British Library

Published by Ladybird Books Ltd
80 Strand London WC2R 0RL
A Penguin Company

4 6 8 10 9 7 5 3

© LADYBIRD BOOKS LTD MM

LADYBIRD and the device of a Ladybird are trademarks of Ladybird Books Ltd

Bella's bedspread

by Mandy Ross
illustrated by Leonie Shearing

introducing the ea spelling of the
short e sound, as in head and bread

Bella had a secret treasure. It was a magic feather bedspread, and it could fly!

Bella's bedspread flew steadily
whatever the weather.

This is heavenly!

Heather Deadwood lived next door to Bella. She was dreadfully jealous of Bella's magic bedspread.

One morning, as Bella got her breakfast ready, Heather crept into Bella's house.

Heather leapt onto Bella's bed. "Get ready bedspread, take it steady bedspread, GO!" she said.

Heather wanted to have a
pleasant ride, but instead…

10

Ooo, my head...

Heather was
soon breathless
and dizzy.

Which just goes to show that jealousy can be very bad for your health.

I feel dreadful...

12

Mr Reardon-Beardon's beard

by Mandy Ross
illustrated by Carla Daly

introducing the **ear** sound,
as in clear and beard

Mrs Reardon-Beardon said,
"Beards are in fashion this year."

"So I hear, my dear,"
said Mr Reardon-Beardon.

So Mr Reardon-Beardon
bought some beard-grower.

He smeared the cream on his
face from
ear to ear

His beard grew...

and grew...

and grew...

until it reached
from here...

to here.

"It's too long, my dear,"
said Mrs Reardon-Beardon, and
she put the beard around
his ears.

"Now I've got an ear-wig,"
said Mr Reardon-Beardon.

"An earwig in your beard?
Oh, dear!" cried
Mrs Reardon-Beardon.

"Not an earwig, my dear," said
Mr Reardon-Beardon more
clearly. "A wig for my ears!"

Christine's
knitted knickers

by Mandy Ross
illustrated by Angie Sage

introducing silent letters

Christine found some balls
of lambswool. They were khaki,
white and red.

"If I knew how to knit, I could knit some knickers," she said.

So she and a friend went to
Knitting School, to find out
what to do.

Geoff soon knitted a woolly
scarf in stitches of red and blue.

"Crumbs – I'm all thumbs and my knitting's in a knot," said Christine getting cross.

Though she soon learned just
how to knit with help
from Mrs Moss.

The finished knickers were rather wrinkled, and the stitches itched a lot.

But they were great for keeping Christine's teapot nice and hot.

Phonics

Learn to read with Ladybird

Phonics is one strand of Ladybird's **Learn to Read** range. It can be used alongside any other reading programme, and is an ideal way to support the reading work that your child is doing, or about to do, in school.

This chart will help you to pick the right book for your child from Ladybird's three main **Learn to Read** series.

Age	Stage	Phonics	Read with Ladybird	Read it yourself
4-5 years	Starter reader	Books 1-3	Books 1-3	Level 1
5-6 years	Developing reader	Books 2-9	Books 4-8	Level 2-3
6-7 years	Improving reader	Books 10-12	Books 9-16	Level 3-4
7-8 years	Confident reader		Books 17-20	Level 4

Ladybird has been a leading publisher of reading programmes for the last fifty years. **Phonics** combines this experience with the latest research to provide a rapid route to reading success.

The fresh, quirky stories in Ladybird's twelve **phonics** storybooks are designed to help your child have fun learning the relationship between letters, or groups of letters, and the sounds they represent.

This is an important step towards independent reading – it will enable your child to tackle new words by 'sounding out' and blending their separate parts.

How **phonics** works

- The stories and rhymes introduce the most common spellings of over 40 key sounds, known as **phonemes**, in a step-by-step way.

- Rhyme and alliteration (the repetition of an initial sound) help to emphasise new sounds.

- Coloured type is used to highlight letter groups, to reinforce the link between spelling and sound:

and the King sang along.

- Bright, amusing illustrations provide helpful picture clues, and extra appeal.

How to use Book 12

The fun stories in this book introduce your child to words including the ear sound, the 'ea' spelling of the short e sound (as in 'bread'), and silent letters. They will help him* begin reading words including these sounds and spellings.

- Read each story through to your child first. Having a feel for the rhythm, rhyme and meaning of the story will give him confidence when he reads it for himself.

- Have fun talking about the sounds and pictures together – what repeated sound can your child hear in *Bella's bedspread*? And in *Mr Reardon-Beardon's beard*?

- Help him break new words into separate sounds (eg. h-ea-d) and blend their sounds together to say the word.

- Point out how words with the same written ending sound the same. If y-ear says 'year', what does he think cl-ear might say?

Some common words, such as 'could', 'some' and even 'the', can't be read by sounding out. Help your child practise recognising words like these so that he can read them on sight, as whole words.

Christine's knitted knickers

This story introduces your child to the idea of silent letters, such as the 'h' in 'white' or the 'w' in 'whole'. The silent letters are picked out in colour. Help your child get to grips with common silent letter spellings, and see if he can think of other examples of words with silent letters in.

The text applies equally to girls and boys, but the child is referred to as 'he' throughout to avoid the use of the clumsy 'he/she'.